Max and Zoe

at Recess

by Shelley Swanson Sateren

illustrated by Mary Sullivan

PICTURE WINDOW BOOKS
a capstone imprint

Max and Zoe is published by Picture Window Books
a Capstone Imprint
1710 Roe Crest Drive
North Mankato, Minnesota 56003
www.capstonepub.com

Library of Congress Cataloging-in-Publication Data
Sateren, Shelley Swanson.
Max and Zoe at recess / by Shelley Swanson Sateren ; illustrated by
Mary Sullivan.
p. cm. -- (Max and Zoe)
Summary: Max always seems to be missing something he needs to
participate in school recess--can his best friend Zoe devise a system
so he will remember everything he needs for school?
ISBN 978-1-4048-7200-4 (library binding)
1. School recess breaks--Juvenile fiction. 2. Schools--Juvenile
fiction. 3. Best friends--Juvenile fiction. [1. Recess--Fiction. 2.
Schools--Fiction. 3. Best friends--Fiction. 4. Friendship--Fiction.]
I. Sullivan, Mary, 1958- ill. II. Title. III. Series: Sateren, Shelley
Swanson. Max and Zoe.

PZ7.S249155Mal 2012
813.54--dc23

2011051236

Designer: Emily Harris

Printed in the United States of America in Stevens Point, Wisconsin.
402012   006678WZF12

Table of Contents

One day, Max and Zoe's teacher, Ms. Young, had a surprise for recess.

"Since it's the first snow of the year, I brought sleds," she said. "Put on your snow gear!"

The class was very excited
and rushed outside.

"Let's ride together, Max,"
said Zoe. "We'll both push
and go super fast."

"Cool," said Max. "This
will be the best recess ever!"

Max and Zoe raced

toward the snowy hill.

"Max," called Ms. Young.

She pointed at his shoes.

"No boots, no playing in the

snow."

"Please?" Max begged.

"Sorry," said Ms. Young. "You have to stay on the playground."

Zoe frowned. "Not again, Max," she said. "You always forget your boots!"

Max hung his head.

"I'm sorry, Max. But I'm

not going to miss sledding,"

Zoe said and ran away.

Max stood on the

playground by himself while

everyone else went sledding.

"Not fair," he thought.

"This is the worst recess

ever!"

Chapter 2
No Shoes

After school, Zoe and Max walked to his apartment.

"No more forgetting your boots," Zoe said. "I have a great idea."

They raced up to Max's room. Zoe found markers and a big piece of paper.

Then she made a giant sign and taped it to Max's door.

"I'll see that every

morning," said Max.

"That's the plan," said

Zoe. "Then you won't

miss any more sledding

adventures."

The next morning, Max

saw the sign.

"My boots!" he said.

He found one boot under

his bed. The other was under

a big pile of clothes.

On the bus, Zoe said,

"The sign worked! You are

wearing your boots."

"I know," said Max. "It's

so cold today. My feet won't

freeze, and I'll get to sled!"

"I can't wait," said Zoe.

That afternoon, Ms.

Young said, "It's too cold to

go outside for recess today.

We'll play parachute games

in the gym instead."

"I love parachute games," said Zoe.

"Me too," said Max.

At the gym door, Ms. Young pointed at Max's feet.

"No boots in the gym," she said.

"Oh, no! I forgot my shoes at home," Max cried.

"Then you'll just have to watch," Ms. Young said.

Max had to sit by the wall the whole time.

After recess, the class

headed back to the room.

"You need to start

remembering your stuff,

Max," Zoe said.

"I know," Max said.

Chapter 3
The List

After school, Zoe and Max

headed to Max's place again.

"I have another idea," Zoe

said. "I need some paper and

a pen."

"Here you go," Max said.

"We need to make a list," Zoe said. "Think of everything you need for school. Then write it down."

1. boots
2. shoes
3. hat
4. mittens
5. snow pants
6. lunch box
7. backpack
8. homework
9. library books

Zoe helped Max search

for everything on the list.

They even found

his missing library

books.

"Wow," said

Max. "I'm ready for school

tomorrow!"

"Just don't forget your backpack," said Zoe.

"No problem," Max said as he hung a new sign on his bedroom door.

The next day at recess, Max and Zoe's class went outside.

Max and Zoe's sled flew down the snowy hill, again and again.

"This is the fastest we've gone yet!" yelled Zoe.

"This is the BEST recess yet!" yelled Max.

About the Author

Shelley Swanson Sateren is the award-winning author of many children's books. She has worked as a children's book editor and in a children's bookstore. Today, besides writing, Shelley works with elementary-school-aged children in various settings. She lives in St. Paul, Minnesota, with her husband and two sons.

About the Illustrator

Mary Sullivan has been drawing and writing her whole life, which has mostly been spent in Texas. She earned her BFA from the University of Texas in Studio Art, but she considers herself a self-trained illustrator. Mary lives in Cedar Park, a suburb of Austin, Texas.

Glossary

adventures (ad-VEN-churz) — exciting experiences

backpack (BAK-pak) — a large bag that you carry on your back

begged (BEGGED) — pleaded with someone to help you

forget (fur-GET) — not remember

parachute (PA-ruh-shoot) — a large piece of strong cloth

recess (REE-sess) — a break from work for rest, play, or relaxation

Discussion Questions

1. With Zoe's help, Max learned ways to remember his school things. Talk about a time you forgot something important.

2. Do you prefer having recess inside the gym or outside on the playground? Why?

3. When Max forgot his boots, he didn't get to play in the snow. Do you think that was fair? Why or why not?

Writing Prompts

1. Make a list of five items you need to bring to school.

2. At recess, Max loves to sled and play parachute games. Write a few sentences about what you like to do at recess.

3. Zoe helps Max learn to remember his things. Write a few sentences about a time when a friend has helped you with something.

Make a Mailbox

There are a lot of things to remember to bring to school. Keeping track of school forms can be tricky. Make an IN mailbox and an OUT mailbox to stay organized.

What you need:

- 2 large cereal boxes, the same size
- light-colored paper, such as yellow or orange
- dark-colored markers, such as blue or green
- scissors
- glue

What you do:

1. Cut out the top of both cereal boxes.

2. Using glue, cover the outside of the boxes with colored paper.

3. Lay the boxes on their backs.

4. On the top of one box, write IN with a marker. Write OUT on the top of the other box.

5. Take school forms out of your backpack. Place them in the IN box. Your parent will sign them and put them in the OUT box.

6. At night, put the finished forms back into your backpack.

The Fun Doesn't Stop Here!

Discover more at www.capstonekids.com

- Videos & Contests
- Games & Puzzles
- Friends & Favorites
- Authors & Illustrators

Find cool websites and more books like this one at www.facthound.com. Just type in the Book ID **9781404872004** and you're ready to go!